I CAN DO IT BY MYSELF

written by
Madison Stokes

pictures by
Sheena Hisiro

A publication of the American Literacy Corporation for Young Readers
Reinforced for Library use

Text copyright © 2010 by Madison Stokes and Floyd Stokes.
Illustrations copyright © 2011 by Sheena Hisiro.
Graphic Design by Sheena Hisiro.
First Edition, 2011. All rights reserved.

ISBN 978-0-9832490-3-0

PRINTED IN CHINA

To my whole family
--Madison

To Paige, Skye and Wade
--Sheena

I can go to sleep myself
I can do it by myself

I can wake up by myself
I can do it by myself

I can brush my teeth myself
I can do it by myself

I can comb my hair myself
I can do it by myself

I can wash my face myself
I can do it by myself

I can button my shirt myself
I can do it by myself

I can beat the drum myself

I can do it by myself

I can eat my food myself
I can do it by myself

I can tie my shoes myself
I can do it by myself

I can kick the ball myself

I can do it by myself

I can ride my bike myself
I can do it by myself

I can take a bath myself
I can do it by myself

I can read my book myself
I can do it by myself

I love to do things by myself. It means that I am learning to be more and more independent. I am able to do things by myself because I practice doing them all the time. You too can do things by yourself if you practice. If there are things that you can't do, don't get frustrated, take your time and keep trying. Eventually, you will be able to do it.

 Madison